Pelts & Promises

Nancy Lohr

Library of Congress Cataloging-in-Publication Data

Lohr, Nancy.
Pelts & promises / Nancy Lohr.
p. cm.
Summary: In 1903, having accidentally ruined the Parson's big pulpit Bible and promised to replace it, Jamie and his best friend Willie B. set out to earn the money by hunting rabbits and selling their pelts.
ISBN 0-89084-899-8 (pbk.)
[1. Moneymaking projects—Fiction. 2. Hunting—Fiction. 3. Country life—Fiction.] I. Title.
PZ7.82895Pe 1997
[Fic]—dc20 96-43861
CIP
AC

Pelts and Promises

Project Editor: Debbie L. Parker

Cover and illustrations by Gabriela Dellosso

Greenville, South Carolina 29614

Printed in the United States of America

ISBN 0-89084-899-8

15 14 13 12 11 10 9 8 7 6 5 4 3 2

To Alan
for encouraging

To Erin
for listening

CONTENTS

Chapter 1

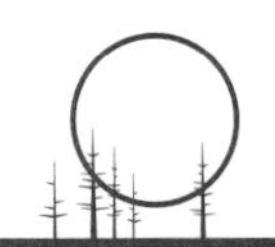

Changing Our World

Willie B. edged toward the schoolhouse and set his dinner pail in the shadow of the steps. He motioned for me to follow.

I put the last wedge of apple into my mouth, wiped the blade of my deerfoot knife on my britches, and slid the knife back into its sheath. I chewed slowly, watching Willie B.

He backed up the stairs, one step at a time, facing the school yard. Something about the set of his jaw reminded me of the time he'd climbed up into the steeple during recess and tied the bell clapper so it couldn't ring.

"Where you going, Willie B.?"

He glanced at me. "Back inside, Jamie. Want to help?"

"With what?"

Willie B. had that look on his face. I'd seen it the time he had wedged part of a cork in the spout on the water pump—and the water sprayed Cassie's dress when she pumped the handle.

I swallowed my apple. "What are you up to now?" I asked. "Will we catch it with Mr. Golde?"

"I'm just going to change my world."

"What?"

"Change my world, Jamie. You know how Mr. Golde was teaching us about inventors today. Edison changed his world. Marconi changed his world. I'm going to change my world. You coming?"

I hesitated, studying Willie B.'s face. Then I took a deep breath of cool autumn air and marched over to the bottom of the steps.

The girls had tied one end of their rope to the fence rail. Callie was turning it for the others, and puffs of dust rose where it slapped the ground. Most of the boys were choosing sides for their noon game, and Mr. Golde was under the pecan tree showing some kids a trick with his handkerchief. No one was watching us.

I ran up the schoolhouse steps three at a time and slipped into the empty schoolroom. It was quiet inside, like on Sunday morning when the preacher opens the big pulpit Bible. Then Willie B. began pushing a table toward the back door. I took the other end to help. The legs scraped the wooden floor with every shove.

Willie B. looked at me. "Open the door. On *three* we'll lift. Ready? *One . . . two . . . three!*"

I hoisted my end above the door sill and wobbled backward down the steps. We moved as quickly as we could across the stubbled grass and set the table down at the edge of the willow trees out back. My hands were sweaty; they get that way when I'm nervous. I wiped them on my britches, adjusted my knife, and then chased Willie B. back to the steps. Willie B. got there first, of course, and jumped up the back steps in one leap.

We made seven other table trips and one more for Mr. Golde's desk. Willie B. acted like we had all the time in the world, but I ran to the window on each return trip just to make sure. Mr. Golde was letting every kid take a turn at the handkerchief trick. We still had time.

We stacked the benches one on top of the other and carried them outside by twos. Then we had only the bookcase and pulpit left. I leaned out the door. Mr. Golde was on his feet, watching the boys' game. "He's looking around."

"Fast," hissed Willie B. "The books." He picked up the empty bookcase, hung it on his right shoulder, and moved heavily down the steps. I followed with a stack of books under one arm and the globe under the other. Willie B. leaned the case against a willow trunk and ran back for the rest of the books, while I jammed mine onto the shelf and set the globe on top.

Only the pulpit now. It was heavier than all the rest of the furniture. We weren't strong enough to lift it, so we had to raise one side at a time and walk it forward. Willie B. kept his hand on the big Bible so it wouldn't fall. We thumped that pulpit down each step and then waggled it back and forth toward the trees. We still had a fair distance to cover when the bell in the top of the steeple began to ring. We pushed the pulpit a few more long waggles, left it at the edge of the grove, and raced around to the front of the schoolhouse.

As the echoes of the bell faded away, we hurried to the end of the line, looking just as sweaty as the ball players.

I never liked waiting on folks to discover one of our plans; it made me nervous, but I had to hand it to Willie B. This prank was pretty good. I couldn't help grinning. I looked down at my hands and picked at a splinter that must have come from the last set of benches.

Mr. Golde gave the usual instructions. "Take your seats and open your readers to today's lesson." The class moved upstairs and entered the back of the room as usual. But just past the coat hooks everyone began bumping together like marbles at the first shot of a game.

Mr. Golde was standing at the back of the group now. "Take your seats," he repeated.

"Someone did," Callie answered.

"Someone did what?" said Mr. Golde.

"Took our seats."

Our teacher pushed his way up the stairs.

He stepped into the schoolroom. The floor sounded hollow under his boots. I wiped my hands on my britches again, then fingered the handle of my knife; I could hear my heart pounding. I watched Mr. Golde turn his head from one side to the other. Every bench was gone; every table was missing; the bookcase had vanished. The globe was gone. Even the front corner where the Sunday pulpit stood was empty. All that was left was the blackboard, the potbellied stove, and the smell of chalkdust in the air. I wiped my hands again.

Slowly Mr. Golde turned; he examined our faces. The others looked as astonished as he. I stared straight down and bumped a pine knot with my toe.

"Willie B.!" Mr. Golde could fire a question and a command in the same word, and he did it now.

"Yes, sir?" answered Willie B. He used his "I have no idea what you mean" voice, and that's when everyone knew that Willie B. had struck again.

"Don't 'yes, sir' me, young man. What is this?"

I looked up at Willie B. He had jammed his hands deep into the pockets of his dungarees, winged his elbows out wide, and was up on his tiptoes. "Just changing my world, sir. You remember. 1879— Edison; 1897— Marconi; 1903— Willie B.! Kind of changes what you think about this old room, doesn't it? I mean, have you ever seen how many knotholes there are in this floor? Have you?"

Was I ever glad to see Mr. Golde's shoulders start to move up and down. His deep laugh was low at first, and then it rumbled up big and loud. Brian and the twins and then the others began to laugh. I was giggling in a relieved kind of way, but Willie B. just plain crowed.

When the laughter finally died away, Mr. Golde cleared his throat and asked, "Then where might our school be?"

"Out back by the willow grove. Jamie and I thought it would be a fine change for our world to take our afternoon session out there."

With a chuckle Mr. Golde said, "Well, boys, you might have something there. We will adjourn to the autumn breezes in the willow grove. Before you two are excused for the day, however—" He paused meaningfully, and I hoped he wouldn't keep us long. Ma expected me right home for chores. "—you will sweep out the schoolhouse." If I got home late, I'd catch certain fury. "Then return all the furniture to the proper places." That was all? I let out the breath I was holding.

"Will do," said Willie B. "Promise."

When school was done for the day, we got the straw brooms and swept up clouds of dust. We pushed our piles of dirt out the back door.

"Open a window, Willie B. I can't breathe."

Willie B. was still pleased with his successful prank and happily opened every window down both sides of the room. A stiff breeze began clearing the air as we hauled the tables and benches back up the steps and put them in place. For the bookshelf, Willie B. said we could leave the books on the shelves and carry the whole thing if we balanced it just right. It took a long time with all the starts and stops, but we did get it back inside that way.

We were going back to the willows for the pulpit when Mr. Golde called out the door. We stopped to listen. "Boys, I don't like to leave you, but I've got to pick up a parcel at the post office before Mrs. Olefson closes the window. I'm expecting those extra primers. Can I trust you two to close up today?"

"Yes, sir," said Willie B.

We walked the pulpit back and forth more slowly this time. Finally we got to the steps and hoisted it up one riser at a time. Once inside, I kicked the door shut with my foot. We put the pulpit in its corner by the window, and straightened the Bible on top.

Willie B. surveyed the room. "That does it."

"You sure, Willie B.?"

"Looks proper to me."

It seemed to me we were forgetting something, but Willie B. picked up his satchel and dinner pail, so I did too. We pulled the front door shut and headed down Morgan's Lane.

The breeze was blowing harder now, chasing the fallen leaves across the road. There was a soft roll of thunder, and we took off running. By the time we parted at the fork, lone raindrops were making puffs on the dusty road.

That was some storm. When the sun came up on Friday morning, heavy drops of rain were still dripping off the bushes and trees, and the smell of damp earth filled the air. Morgan's Lane was one long puddle.

I got to school before Willie B., and I discovered what we had forgotten the day before. The windows. The rain had poured through the open windows, soaked the pine benches, and formed sooty pools around the stove.

I knew Mr. Golde would have to scold us, and sure enough, as soon as Willie B. came through the door, Mr. Golde spoke. But his voice didn't sound regular. It was real stern, real soft.

"William Bartholomew. James. I will see you at my desk immediately."

Sounded like something worse than windows, but I couldn't think what else we had done.

"I told you to close up properly."

Willie B. began to look around the room, searching for the problem. "Yes, sir, you did. And I gave you my word."

"Then I'm afraid your word just isn't good enough. Look at this."

In Mr. Golde's hand was a dripping wet book. It was the Parson's big pulpit Bible.

Chapter 2

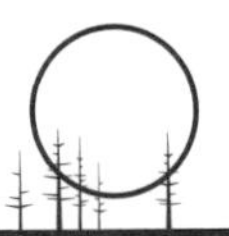

The Damage Is Done

Willie B. looked at the Bible, at Mr. Golde, and then back at the Bible. I looked at Willie B.

"Explain the destruction of this book, boys."

Willie B. is honest, at least. "I'm sorry, Mr. Golde. We didn't shut the windows like we should have, but I didn't know rain was coming, truly. I'm sorry. Really, I am. It'll dry out, won't it?"

I swallowed hard and wiped my hands on my britches. I just kept looking at Willie B.

Mr. Golde took three slow steps to his table at the front of the room. He set the Bible down like it was a fancy china cup, then he moved to his chair and sat. A puddle formed around the Bible. When he finally lifted his face, his eyes looked as hard as steel marbles.

"You two know how much I care for the books we have in this room. We've worked to keep them clean, to keep them . . ." His voice trailed off.

He cleared his throat and started again. "But to cause harm to God's Word. I can't tell you what that does to me. I'm afraid, William and James, that a simple apology just won't be enough this time. Set this room to rights, immediately. Dry the benches at once and mop the floor. And I will see you both at recess about the rest."

We answered together, our voices low. "Yes, sir." The bucket and cleaning rags were by the back door, and we wasted no time. We were in serious trouble, and I knew that when my pa heard about this, it would go even worse for me.

Even though Willie B. and I were the ones in trouble, everybody was quiet and well behaved all morning.

When Mr. Golde dismissed the class for noon recess, the others ran out the door and clattered down the wooden steps.

Mr. Golde reached for the wet Bible. Willie B. and I stood and watched. The cover curled open softly like Ma's dishrag. He tried to turn the first page, but it lifted right out in his hand. He set the loose page back in its place and turned to the center of the book. He handled the page gently, but the paper between his thumb and fingers pulled free like a little moon. He laid down the crescent and slowly rose from his chair. "It is ruined."

I had to say something. "We're sorry, Mr. Golde. Please forgive us. We'll buy a new Bible, Willie B. and I, we will." Willie B. nodded.

No answer. I reached out for Mr. Golde's arm as he passed.

He stopped and looked directly into my eyes. "I am sorely disappointed in both of you, but I will accept your apology. As far as the ruined Bible is concerned, . . . well, that's a matter to settle with your parents and the Parson. You'll have to make your peace with them."

"But the Parson was just here on Sunday," Willie B. said. "He won't be back in our pulpit until late October. That's too long."

"Maybe some time to think will do you boys good." He turned and walked out of the schoolhouse without another word.

We followed slowly behind. When I got to the bottom of the steps, my knees buckled and I sat down hard. Willie B. sat down beside me. He pulled his sandwich out of his dinner pail and took a bite. I wondered how he could eat. Ma had packed a ham biscuit and a pickle in my pail—my favorite lunch—but I wasn't hungry, even for that.

Finally I said, "What are we going to do now?"

Willie B. swallowed the food in his mouth, then started talking, slowly at first, then faster as he went along. "I've been thinking on that. First we have to tell our folks and get our lickings out of the way. Then we have to earn some money and buy the Parson a new Bible."

He said that like it was going to be as easy as gathering eggs from sleeping chickens. "Earn money?" I exclaimed. "Willie B., we're just kids. You know that neither your pa nor mine will pay for choring." My voice was getting higher the longer I talked. "Who do we know that could pay us for anything?" I was shaking now and gulping for air.

"Now stop it, Jamie. We'll think of something. If we can't earn any money, then I'll just . . . well, I'll just sell Dog. She's a good hunting dog, and she'd probably bring enough to pay for a new Bible."

I knew that the day Willie B. gave up Dog would be the day I'd give up my deerfoot knife I'd won in the Spelling Bee.

I can still remember the day two years back when we'd heard Dog whimper. We figured she was just a little runt left to die, and we went into the timber to find her. Before I had a chance to claim her as my own, Willie B. had cradled that little white pup into his shirt and carried her out of there. As fast as anything, Willie B. was just gone on her. He'd fed her and loved her and taught her to hunt, even though no one knew if she was the kind of dog that could learn hunting.

Every time I watched her trotting into the bushes, holding that white tail high, I'd think—I'd dream—*Someday I'll have a dog like her to call my own.*

And here lately Willie B. had been thinking she was going to have pups. No. He couldn't sell Dog, and that was that.

I fingered the handle of my knife and thought about all kinds of ways to make money, but as my ma says, none of them held any promise.

By the time we walked down Morgan's Lane that afternoon, the puddles had shrunk into little circles of water. We didn't talk. I guess we were both figuring out what to say when we got home. At least I know I was, and I felt sick in the bottom of my stomach.

At the fork, we looked at each other, and then without a word walked off.

When I got home, Ma was in her garden, picking the last beans of the season. She sat back on her heels and waved to me. "Fresh cookies on the table, Jamie. Milk's in the icebox. I'll be in soon."

I waved feebly. "Thanks, Ma." At the porch I kicked the dirt off my boots and went into the kitchen. I set my dinner pail on the drain board and then carried my satchel up to my room. The cookies smelled good, but I wasn't hungry. I walked out to the barn and found Pa, right where I knew he'd be.

I took a deep breath that tasted of straw and harness leather.

"Pa." It came out like a question.

"Hello, Jamie. How was your day?"

I got right to the point. "Well, sir, it wasn't so good and I need to talk to you about it."

Pa stopped working on the harness and slung it over a peg. "Sounds serious." He upturned a bucket and sat down.

"Yes, sir. It is that." I told Pa everything, starting with the part about changing our world and the way Mr. Golde had laughed at our prank, only it didn't seem so funny now. I told him about leaving the windows open and then the rain. My voice was getting high. I stopped and swallowed the big lump in my throat; I didn't know how to go on.

The bucket creaked as Pa leaned forward; I could feel his breath. "And the rain ruined something. Is that it?"

I nodded.

"Is that it?" He was louder this time; he expected me to speak.

"Yes, sir."

"Ruined what?"

"Parson's Bible. I'm sorry Pa. I didn't mean to do harm."

He spoke slowly, one word at a time. "Meaning and doing are two different things. Get the belt."

I knew better than to argue; I hurried over to the barn wall. Next to all the harness straps was my strap. I lifted the wide piece of leather off the peg, then hustled back across the barn and handed the strap to Pa. I knew what to do, and so did Pa.

Chapter 3

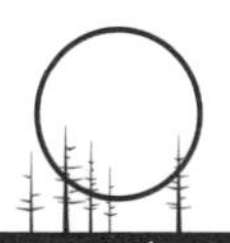

Our Fathers Speak

After dinner we went to see Willie B. and his pa.

It looked like Willie B.'s licking had been as hard as mine. He walked out of the house real slow, and I could see where the tears had washed white streaks down his cheeks. My pa pointed to the top rail on the fence, and we both sat there, carefully. Then Pa offered his hand to Willie B.'s father.

After they'd shaken hands, my pa spoke. "Looks like these boys got themselves into real serious trouble, William. They promised Mr. Golde they'd buy a new Bible. That'll cost a good bit, I'd guess. Money I don't have. Even if I did, I can't pay Jamie to do chores that have to be done anyway."

I looked sideways at Willie B. He was about as serious as I'd ever seen him. I fingered the handle of my deerfoot knife.

"So, I guess these boys have their work set out for them," my pa said. "They need to make good on their word and pay their vow like it says in the Bible. They can learn what Ecclesiastes 5:5 means. Have you got any thoughts?"

Willie B.'s dad looked at the two of us on the fence rail before answering. "Was up in Madison the end of last week. Saw a sign in the General Store. Firm out east's buying pelts. Your boy hunt?"

"Jamie has done some—with my Winchester. I'd be willing for him to use it."

Willie B.'s dad glanced back at us. "Sell pelts, you two?"

"That's fine," I said, but I didn't figure it really mattered what we thought. "What about bullets, Pa?"

"Under the circumstances, I think you two should buy your own bullets. That's about a penny a shot."

I liked to hunt and so did Willie B., but this sure wasn't the way I wanted to do it. We couldn't afford to miss.

The four of us worked it all out. Willie B. and I would hunt rabbits with my pa's rifle; I had my knife for skinning them, and Willie B.'s pa would take us to Madison to sell the pelts. Our mothers could have all the meat.

My pa reached out his hand again. "Thank you, William. Sorry to take your time on such matters."

The two men moved away from the fence, and I turned to Willie B., my teeth clenched. "Willie B., this is the worst trouble I've ever been in and I want out, fast. Tomorrow we hunt."

Chapter 4

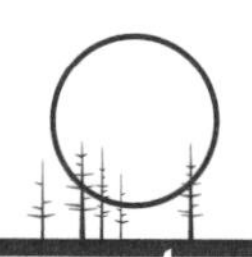

The Game Hunts Begin

I had a twenty-five cent piece I'd been saving for the future, but we needed shells now. So I put my coin on the Mercantile counter along with Willie B.'s nickels and pennies.

Mr. Olefson drew our money across the counter one coin at a time. "Twenty-five, thirty; thirty-five, forty; forty-one, forty-two, and forty-three. That's good, boys. One box of shells." Mr. Olefson leaned his blond head way over until he was nose-to-nose with Willie B. "A lot of bullets for boys, don't you think? Going to war, are you?" Then he straightened up and laughed at his own joke.

"No, sir." Willie B. had his hands in his pockets like he was the owner of this very Mercantile. "We're going to be hunting rabbits and selling skins in Madison." He made it sound like we thought this up as a lark. You'd never have known we were paying the biggest debt of our lives.

"And don't you worry, Mr. Olefson, we'll spend all of our money right here." Willie B. tapped the counter with his finger.

I reached out for the box of shells and began to move away. "Come on, Willie B.; we can't waste a whole Saturday in here."

"Just a minute, Jamie. One more thing, Mr. Olefson. What do you think it would cost to buy a new Bible?"

The blond eyebrows shot up. "A Bible, Willie B.?"

"Yes, sir. Anything wrong with a boy buying a Bible?"

I could tell that Mr. Olefson thought we were up to something and he probably ought to stop us. "What size?" He didn't take his eyes off us, even while he reached into his catalog drawer.

"Oh, pretty big. About the size of the Parson's Bible." Willie B.'s elbows winged out like they do when he's got someone going, and his smile was growing bigger.

"The Parson need a new Bible?"

"Guess a preacher couldn't ever have too many."

Mr. Olefson plumped a thick catalog onto the counter. He stopped asking questions, but he didn't stop looking puzzled. He ran his finger down a page, stopped on a number, then flipped some pages. He read for a minute. "If two boys were buying a parson's Bible, it would cost them ten dollars and ninety-eight cents. Anything else?"

"Thank you, Mr. Olefson. That's all I need to know. You want anything else, Jamie?"

He knew I only wanted to get out of the Mercantile.

"Let's go, Willie B. We've got to get started."

Dog was waiting on the porch. She danced down the steps beside him. To look at these two, you'd think we were off to the Harvest Fair.

When we were finally out of town and hiking toward Beamer's Pond, I slowed down. Ten dollars and ninety-eight cents!

"Willie B." My voice rose. "We can't earn ten dollars and ninety-eight cents! That's a fortune. Pa gave thirteen dollars for Ma's cook stove!"

"Stop it, Jamie. What else can we do? We told Mr. Golde we'd buy a new Bible; we gave our word."

"Then Mr. Golde was right—our word isn't worth very much."

We never really fight, Willie B. and I, but we didn't talk the rest of the way out to the pond. Willie B. carried the rifle in the crook of his right elbow. I carried the box of shells, and I walked as far away from Willie B. as two boys can get on one path.

Dog kept nosing her snout into Willie B.'s open hand. She always knew when something was wrong.

We were walking fast and were pretty winded when we got to the north end of the pond. Then we stopped and just looked at each other. Neither of us said a word. Willie B. didn't want to ask for a bullet, and I didn't want to offer one.

Pretty soon I started thinking about who would talk first, and I began to giggle. Dog nudged Willie B. in the stomach. He's real ticklish—and well—we both broke out laughing. I don't know how long we rolled around under the trees, but I do know we were friends again when we finally stood up.

I offered Willie B. a shell. "Want the first shot?"

He loaded the Winchester and stepped out in front of the trees. He looked down at Dog prancing beside him. "Dog. Rabbits." And she was off. I've never seen any dog hunt that way, but after all she is Willie B.'s dog.

She flushed out a big, brown hare right away. Willie B. drew a bead on that rabbit and followed her. He squeezed off the round, but the hare darted back into the brush.

He reloaded, and Dog ran again. After five shots, he had two rabbits. He hung them on his belt, then handed the Winchester to me.

I knew Dog wouldn't run for me, so I walked around to the clearing behind the blackberry brambles. I crept up to my favorite spot; then with the rifle ready, I ran alongside the brambles. It worked. I flushed out two big ones on that first try.

I knelt down and braced my arm on my leg; my pa hates to see me shoot that way, but it helps my aim. I got the rabbit in my sights, held my breath, and squeezed the trigger. It turned a somersault in the air and tumbled to a stop. Pa's Winchester is a single shot rifle, so I had to let the other hare go while I reloaded. I collected my rabbit, tied it to my belt, and ran at another bramble.

I couldn't raise anything. I kneeled down and watched, but nothing else ran into the clearing.

After a while we stopped to eat the bread and apples Ma had packed for us. Then Willie B. loaded up to try again. He sent Dog out, but it looked like every rabbit in this neck of the woods was going to wait us out.

The sun had already passed overhead, so we pocketed our spent shells and carried the three rabbits back to Willie B.'s.

There was a plank shelf on the back of his barn, and we laid the rabbits out on it. I pulled my knife out of its sheath. Pa had helped me sharpen the blade at his wheel, and I circled the skin around the paws as easy as slicing butter. I glanced up at Willie B. "Be careful now; a good clean pelt will bring a better price."

With his pa's blade, Willie B. cut the underside open and cleaned out each animal. I made straight cuts up the legs, and we both peeled the skins off like little fur jackets. While Willie B. took the meat to his ma, I began scraping the inside of one pelt. When he came back, we both scraped. It took a long time before the pelts were clean and trimmed. Willie B. stretched each one like a miniature bear rug up high on the barn wall, and I nailed them tight.

We drew a bucket of water, rinsed our hands and knives, then dropped down into the dust by the barn to look up at our three pelts. They reminded me of three little lily pads on a big pond. I turned my knife end for end and with the deer's foot started drawing figures in the dust.

"Changing your world, Jamie?"

I threw a clod of dirt at him. "Not funny, Willie B. I think we changed ours for a long time to come. Look at this."

I scratched $10.98 in the dirt. "If we can get twenty cents each for these pelts, then we still need ten dollars and thirty-eight cents."

I looked at Willie B. "Do you realize how long it's going to take us at this rate?"

He studied the numbers in the dirt. "I guess the rest of the school year."

"Rest of the school year! We'll be lucky if we aren't growing beards by the time we buy that new Bible! That is—if we live through telling the Parson."

Dog rested her nose on Willie B.'s knee and looked right at him. And for once Willie B. had nothing to say.

Chapter 5

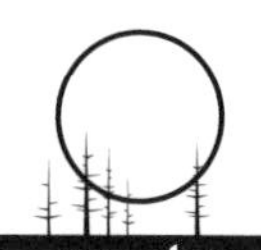

The Parson Speaks

The Parson's circuit wouldn't bring him back to our church until the fourth Sunday of October. The almanac said the days were getting shorter, but by my way of reckoning they were plenty long, waiting to tell the Parson.

When that Sunday finally arrived, seemed like it took Ma forever to get the dinner basket filled.

"Jamie." She stopped and frowned at me while she held a cake over the basket. "Please go on outside."

"I'm just trying to help."

"You'll help me by getting out from underfoot. You've waited a whole month to talk to the Parson. What are a few minutes more?"

Forever, I thought, but I walked outside. I kicked at a rock with one foot, and then with the other. Left, right, left, right. I wondered if I could kick it between the wagon wheels. The rock sailed into the air and thumped against the leg of Traveler, our horse. With a sharp whinny she pulled away from the fence rail until her harness held her tight.

"Jamie!" Pa was immediately at Traveler's side. "Whoa, girl; easy now. Jamie, you get in the wagon and settle yourself down."

Finally our wagon rounded the bend on Morgan Lane. I was watching for the Parson, a round, ruddy giant of a man. There he was at the top of the schoolhouse steps, shaking hands with everyone—the men, the women, even the children. He had a powerful grip. Pa said this was one parson who could bring a man to his knees with his handshake. I followed Ma and Pa up the steps and waited my turn.

"Good morning, Mrs. Refsell, Mr. Refsell," Parson said. "How are you both this fine Lord's Day?"

I didn't hear their answers. I was rehearsing my words one more time. I looked up into his clear blue eyes.

"Good morning, Jamie." He squeezed my hand and patted my head.

"Morning, Parson. I'm sorry about this news, but—"

"Good morning, Mr. Olefson." The Parson had reached out his hand to Mr. Olefson, behind me.

I stepped around Mr. Olefson for another try. "Parson, the pulpit Bible is gone and I have to talk to you about it."

The Parson looked down at me. Wrinkles drew across his forehead. "Oh?" The lines eased. "Oh, you've taken it home to begin work on your Christmas reading. Good boy, Jamie. I knew I could count on you."

We were blocking the door and other folks were waiting.

We sang every verse of every song—slowly. Then the Parson preached on the Lord's harvest day. He lifted his own small Bible in the air as he preached.

I met Willie B. after the service. "So what'd he say?"

"Too busy with the others, Willie B. Maybe he'll listen now."

"Parson?" Willie B. spotted him first, over where the ladies were laying out the food.

"Just a minute boys; let me help the men with these tables."

I had no more minutes. "Please, Parson, now?" My voice was high. He turned, looked into our faces, and then walked our way.

Although we hadn't worked it out together, Willie B. and I alternated telling parts of the story until I told about the ruined Bible. The Parson didn't think much of pranks. I could remember times he had preached about foolishness.

"We're already hunting, and we'll sell our pelts to buy a new Bible," I said. "We'll have the new Bible by the end of the school term at the rate we're getting pelts, and Pa said we'll know the meaning of Ecclesiastes 5:5 by then too. Keeping our vow, that is."

The Parson fixed his left hand on Willie B.'s shoulder and his right hand on mine. His grip was as firm as his handshake. "I'm sure your fathers have punished you for your foolishness, so I'll consider that part of this prank settled, young men."

His red face was serious. "And buying the new Bible is the proper way to make restitution." I wiped my hands on my Sunday pants as he paused. "But I must insist on having the new Bible in time for

Christmas. You both know that in our pageant, one wise man always carries the Holy Scriptures and reads Luke's account of the blessed birth."

He looked into my eyes. "I chose you to be that wise man this year, Jamie."

I swallowed and nodded.

"Have you boys thought about what Jamie will carry?" he asked. "What Jamie will read? What Jamie will lay at the foot of the manger?"

His questions tumbled one after the other into my ears. I hadn't thought about *those* things, and I sure couldn't now.

"He could use his pa's Bible or yours," said Willie B.

The Parson didn't answer right off. His hand on my shoulder was as heavy as a sack of flour, and the silence in the air was just as heavy.

Finally the Parson cleared his throat and pulled his hands away. "No, Willie B. You will both still be wise men, and Jamie will read from the new pulpit Bible, or the two of you will explain the whole matter to the church."

Chapter 6

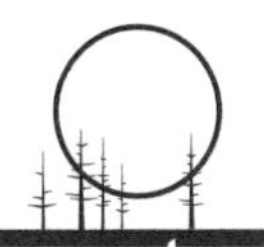

Trading Day

Since we had chores to do every day, we could hunt only on Saturdays. Willie B. called them our game hunt days, and we tried to enjoy them, but I didn't have much fun knowing that neither the skins nor the money were ours for keeps.

Willie B.'s pa said a trip to Madison would have to be worth his time. He told us he'd make the first trip when we had twenty pelts, so we counted the skins on the barn regular as clockwork.

Our first trading day finally arrived the Saturday after we talked to the Parson. Trip or no trip, chores had to be done; so I got up early to finish mine. The chickens came last. I scattered feed in their yard, filled the water pans, and then gathered eggs from the coop.

I could smell Ma's cookies before I saw them. She was putting the last ones on a plate when I came in with the eggs. I set the basket on the drain board; Ma took me by the shoulders and turned me to face her.

"Is everything done?"

"Yes, Ma, until evening chores."

"Will your jacket be warm enough?"

"I think so. I have my flannel shirt on too."

"That's good. There should be plenty of food for both your dinner and supper." A trip to Madison and back took a full day. "And I put in extra cookies, enough for all three of you. Better be on your way." She kissed the top of my head and reached for the lunch basket. "We'll be praying for you, Jamie. Be anxious to hear how well you do."

"Thanks, Ma."

I hurried out to the fork to wait for Willie B. and his pa to come along.

I saw the dust from their wagon first. When they got close, Willie B.'s pa slowed his horse, but he didn't stop. I clambered into the wagon as Dog barked a greeting. Willie B. patted the bundle of pelts. "Payday, Jamie! Feels good, doesn't it?"

"I guess so, but I sure wish this was our last trip and not our first."

"Ah, you worry too much. We'll do fine." Willie B. settled back on some empty grain sacks, pulled his harmonica from his overalls pocket, and started blowing out a tune.

I lay back too, and watched the autumn leaves pass overhead. I could make out pictures where the sky broke through.

We rattled on down the road for a while. Willie B. had stopped working on his harmonica and was resting with his head on his hands. Dog had her snout wedged in under his elbow. Her belly was bulging with the growing puppies.

Willie B.'s pa was quiet like usual. Finally he pulled the wagon off the road, turned around on his seat, and held out a jug. "Go for water, boys." Stopping for cold spring water was one of the best parts about a trip to Madison.

Before I could even stand up, Willie B. had snatched the jug. "Beat you." He jumped over the side of the wagon and took off for the spring. Dog lumbered along behind.

We ate quickly without any chatter and then got back into the wagon for the rest of the drive. The sun was straight overhead when Willie B.'s pa tied up in front of the General Store. "Be back here before one on the bank clock. My trading won't take any longer than that."

By the time I had adjusted my deerfoot knife and picked up the roll of skins, Willie B. and Dog were already out of the wagon. Willie B.'s boots struck the wooden porch confidently. Out front, there were all sizes of signs tacked to the wall.

"Here it is. *Will buy pelts—large or small. Prices fair. Inquire within.* What's that mean?"

"Ask. You doing the talking?"

"Of course. We want a good price, don't we?" His hands were stuck deep in his pockets, and I figured he'd get the job done. "Stay, Dog."

She dropped down beside a bench, and I pushed open the door. A little bell at the top of the door jingled. There were a couple of men at a checkerboard in the back; they turned to look at us.

Off to our right, the storekeeper himself stood behind the counter. "May I help you two?" He had a bushy black mustache that curled up on the ends.

"We'd like to do some trading," said Willie B.

"Did you hear that, boys?" The storekeeper called to the checker players. "These two want to do some trading."

The others laughed, and one of them said, "Careful now, Bob. Don't let them put you out of business." They laughed some more.

The mustache talked to us again. "So, what have you two got?"

"The sign says—" Willie B. nodded to the porch "—you'll buy pelts. We've got twenty good rabbit skins we'd be willing to sell."

"Lay them out and let's have a look-see."

I cut the string tied around our bundle and spread out the skins on the man's counter. He picked them up one at a time, measured them with his hand, and checked for bullet holes. He knew skins; you could tell by the way he looked them over. Finally he turned back to us. "This is fine craftsmanship, boys. Who helped you?"

"No one, sir," Willie B. said. "This is our own work. So, how much will you give?"

"Let's slow down now."

"No time to go slow, sir. Name your price, or we'll need to move on to a serious buyer."

The man was sizing us up. I figured he just might tell us to move on, and he was sure to know we didn't have another buyer. "Now, Willie B., give the man some time to think."

"Thank you, Son. I appreciate your consideration. Truth is, these are nice pelts and should bring a good price. I can give you five dollars for the lot. Is that good enough?"

I could see Willie B. getting ready to wrangle, so I jumped in again. "Why, that would be fine, sir." I hoped the man didn't notice my voice going up. "That's twenty-five cents a pelt, Willie B. That's real fair! Now isn't it?"

Willie B. rubbed his chin with his fingers. "I don't know." I stepped on his foot and glared at him. "Oh, I suppose it's fair enough." Willie B. looked directly at the storekeeper. "That is, I'll settle for five dollars so long as we can count on you to buy some more—next time we come to town."

The mustache widened as he smiled. "Businessmen, I see. Well, if your work is as well done next time, I'd be proud to trade with you if I can. How do you want your money? In goods?" He bundled the skins back together and set them aside.

"Hard cash, please." Willie B.'s hand was already palm up on the counter.

We were back in the road by the wagon with time to spare. Dog was scratching her back in the dust at Willie B.'s feet.

"I got us a good price, didn't I?"

"You almost lost us the whole sale! He offered us top dollar, and you were ready to walk away. A serious buyer? Who are you trying to fool?"

"Ah, I was just bluffing; you can't take the first price you're offered."

"You can if it's better than the best we ever hoped for!"

"You're just sore that I finished a good deal." Willie B. pushed my shoulders with both his hands. I shoved him back against the hitching rail and before I knew what was happening, he'd dropped me to the dust and pinned me down. Dog was barking and dancing around us in a wide circle.

"Trading done?" Willie B.'s pa stood on the wooden walk a step above the road.

We untangled ourselves and smacked the dust off our overalls. Willie B. grinned at me.

"Done and done, Pa. Look." He drew the coins out of his pocket and cupped them in his hand.

"A good day's work. Into the wagon, boys."

The trip home was just backward from the morning, except we didn't talk at all. I ran my finger up and down the deerfoot sticking out of its sheath and thought about our money. Willie B. wheezed in and out on his harmonica until his pa told him to put it away. The sun was almost down by the time we got to the fork.

"You keep the money, Jamie."

I scooped the coins out of Willie B.'s hand. "Thanks, Willie B. I'll put it in the jar on our mantle. And I guess you did get us a good price." I grabbed Ma's empty basket and jumped off the end of the moving wagon.

Chapter 7

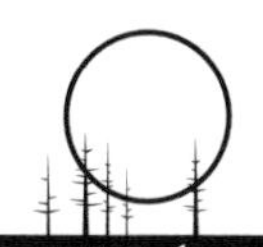

The Trouble with Dog

On Monday, Willie B. didn't meet me at the fork, so I walked to school alone.

The school yard was noisy by the time I arrived, and I looked all around but I couldn't see him. Mr. Golde rang the bell, and we all filed in.

Then like always, he called each name on the roll. Everyone knew that Willie B. never missed school, so we all turned when he didn't answer his name.

Mr. Golde looked up too, and raised his eyebrows. He hadn't brought up the Bible again since that first day, but I knew he sure didn't trust us yet either. "William Bartholomew?" He scanned the room to see if Willie B. was hiding somewhere. "Does anyone know the whereabouts of young Willie B.?"

We shrugged our shoulders and looked at each other.

"Any of you see him this weekend?"

I spoke up. "Yes, sir. His pa took us to Madison on Saturday, and Willie B. was just fine then."

"Thank you, Jamie. Well, I expect we can manage without him for once. Take out your readers and begin today's lesson."

By the end of the day I was sure something had to be wrong with Willie B. I ran down Morgan's Lane, figuring how fast I could get my chores done. Surely then Ma would let me check on him. At the fork I stopped. Maybe I should go first and then get on home. Yes. That was the thing to do; I hurried on.

At Willie B.'s I didn't see anyone outside, so I stepped onto his porch and knocked on the door. I could hear brisk footsteps, and then Willie B.'s ma opened the door. She gave my shoulder a squeeze like she always does.

"Well, hello, Jamie. I heard you boys made out real well in Madison. Why, five dollars is a handsome sum of money for young boys to earn."

"Yes, ma'am—"

"I told William that it was a splendid start to sell your pelts for such a good price. It certainly made the long trip to Madison well worth the time, now didn't it?"

"Yes, ma'am. How's Willie B.?"

"Fine, just fine. How kind of you to ask."

"What I mean is . . . well, he wasn't at school, and I just thought maybe he was sick."

"Well, of course. That is just what you would mean, isn't it? No, he's fine. Dog isn't real perky, though. It's time for her pups. I keep telling him they will come whether he stews or not, but you know my Willie B. He sets great store by that animal, and she's not having an easy time of it. He even talked his father into letting him stay out of school today to tend that dog. Oh, there's my teakettle. He's out in the barn, Jamie."

She bustled off to the kitchen, and I hopped down from the porch and ran to the barn. When I stopped just inside the door to get used to the dim light, I could hear Willie B. I followed the sound of his voice and found him by the ladder below the loft. Dog was lying on her side in a bed of fresh hay, her nose on Willie B.'s leg. He was stroking her head and talking gently to her.

I knelt down in front of them and reached out to pat Dog. She raised her head, bared her teeth, and growled at me. I snatched my hand back.

"Leave her alone, Jamie!"

"What's wrong?"

"She's hurting; now leave her alone. Pa says sometimes the first litter is real hard on a dog."

"Did you call for Doc Carlson?"

Willie B. didn't answer.

"Well, did you?"

He scrubbed the back of his hand across his eyes and shook his head no.

Dog began to moan, and Willie B. stroked her head. "It's all right, girl. You'll be all right." She began to tremble, and the moans turned into little yelps.

"I'll get Doc." I was on my feet.

"No, Jamie."

That wasn't what I expected from him. "Why not?"

He took a deep breath. "Doc has to charge, and there's no money for that." He turned back to Dog and rubbed one of her ears between his fingers.

I made myself offer. "What about our money?"

Slowly he looked up at me. "Pa said no. That money's already spent. Said whatever happens, happens." A tear rolled down his cheek.

"Then I'll get your pa." And I didn't wait for him to answer.

Willie B.'s pa lowered himself down into the hay and put his big hand on Dog. She growled at him too, but he didn't move. He spoke real low, and though I couldn't hear what he was saying, Dog quieted down.

"Boys—clean rags." We were off like a shot.

When we got back, Willie B.'s pa had one hand on Dog's back and was rubbing her swollen belly with the other.

"Pa. Don't hurt her."

"Got to turn this pup, son. Hold her head."

Willie B. sat back down and cradled her head. There was nothing for me to do. Between the two of them, they worked for a long while to turn that pup. Dog made soft moaning sounds.

I didn't hear Willie B.'s ma come into the barn. "Jamie. Do you know what time it is?"

"No, ma'am. What?"

"It's getting late, and your mama won't hold supper much longer. You'd better move along."

"Can't I stay until the puppies are born?"

"William? How much longer do you think it will be?"

Willie B.'s pa looked up at me. "Long. Best be going."

When I stepped outside, I saw that the sun was already going down. Supper was not going to be my biggest problem. I ran. When I got home, Ma was by the gate to the pigpen.

"Well, look who's here." I could tell her jaw was set; she was angry. "And just where have you been?"

"Ma, I can explain."

"You had chores to do."

"Ma, I'm sorry. It's just that Dog is having trouble with her puppies, and I stayed to help. I should have come right home. I know that; I'm sorry. I won't ever do it again."

"Well, I'm glad you're sorry, but we are counting on you around here. For the next full week you will have some additional chores to remind you of that."

"I could feed the pigs for you now."

"I've fed them."

I went into the house. Pa was in his chair reading. He looked up at me and raised one eyebrow. "See your ma?" I nodded. "Well, enough said then. Better eat." A plateful of cold food sat on the table.

In the morning Ma piled my breakfast plate with pancakes and put another stack in front of Pa. I dove right in. "Slow down there." She pulled my plate away. "Running off to school early won't do the first thing to help Willie B. and that dog of his." She slid the plate back into place.

I tried to eat slowly, but I made the bites real big. When I was done, I carried my empty plate to the drain board. Ma took my shoulders and turned me to see if I had washed my neck and ears. Finally she handed me my dinner pail. "You'll be home in time for chores today?"

"To be sure, Ma."

"That's good." She smiled at me. "Give me a reason to do some baking today."

I took off running. Willie B. wasn't at the fork today either, but I waited just the same. I paced back and forth from my road to his. I waited for the longest time, until I just knew I had to start on to school alone. I walked backwards watching for him, but when he hadn't come by the time I got to the bend, I turned and ran the rest of the way to school. The yard was already empty, and I took the steps three at a time. I slipped onto my bench just as Mr. Golde called my name.

The morning was half over by the time we had finished our reading lessons. Then Mr. Golde started drilling us on our figures. My turn came, and I stood. He liked to give us problems that were hard to cipher. "Jamie, give us the sum of . . ." He looked out the window, turned back to me and smiled. "Jamie, I do believe you ought to go outside and fill our water bucket."

"Sir?"

He laughed a little. "Water, Jamie, water. We're thirsty."

I was puzzled, but I picked up the water bucket, walked out the back door of the schoolhouse and over to the pump. I was just lifting the handle when I looked up and saw Willie B. sauntering up Morgan's Lane, big as life. His hands were in his pockets and his elbows were winged way up high.

"Willie B.!" I dropped the pump handle and took out after him. By the time I reached him, I was out of breath and panting. "How is she?"

He didn't answer right off; and when he did, his words came out slowly. "Dog is a mama, Jamie." He sounded just like my pa after a long calving—gentle, but pleased. "Yes, sir. One boy and a little lady."

Chapter 8

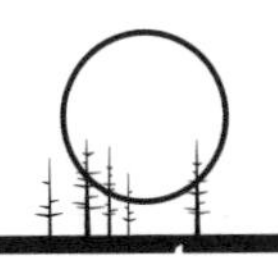

More Pelts to Sell

Ma did keep her word about those extra chores. Every day I worked after school until supper and then after supper until dark. I figured I wouldn't get to see Dog's pups until their eyes were open.

It was on Saturday that Ma said, "You'd best check on Dog and then get on about replacing the Parson's Bible. You can hunt until evening chores."

"Thanks, Ma! I'll be back on time." I strapped on my knife, picked up the box of shells, shouldered Pa's rifle, and pounded down the path. I knew where I'd find Willie B., so I didn't bother knocking at the house.

Sure enough. He was in the barn same as last time, only now Dog was nestled up against him and her pups against her.

"Will she let me touch them?"

"Sure, but talk to her first. Let her know you won't hurt them."

I laid the rifle in the hay, and knelt down slowly. I greeted Dog softly, then I reached out my hand for her to sniff. I stroked the top of her head and down onto her back. Then I slid my hand over to the black puppy. Dog didn't object. The puppy was softer than corn silk, only it was warm and full of life.

"What did you name them?"

"Been working on that, but nothing fits yet. Pa said I can't keep them, so I oughtn't get attached. He said one dog is all we need."

I need a dog, I thought. Oh, how many times have I told Pa that I need a dog? I fingered the wrinkled skin of the puppy. Aloud I said, "This pup is softer than our very best pelt."

Pelts! I thought. "Game hunt, Willie B.!"

"Game hunt?"

I guess I surprised him as much as I did myself.

"Ma said I could hunt today."

"Well, you can hunt all you want, but I'm staying with Dog."

Maybe it was mean, but I knew a way to get him on his feet. I smiled. "Fine. We can sell pelts or we can sell Dog. Take your pick." I waited while he blinked and swallowed twice.

Willie B. nuzzled each of the puppies in turn before setting them gently at Dog's side. He scratched Dog behind the ears, then lifted her muzzle with one hand. "Got promises to keep, girl."

Without another word, he stood and dusted himself off. "Game hunt, Jamie."

And it was a good one. I got six rabbits and only wasted two shots. Willie B. did nearly as well, even without Dog.

"Let's nail them in rows of four, Jamie."

"Why?"

"Well, four pelts will bring one dollar. We can count it up real easy that way."

So I nailed up two rows and part of the next and was home in time for chores. All told, it was a pretty good day.

After two more hunts we had five rows of pelts on the barn. We pulled the nails, rolled up the skins, and headed back to Madison. When I climbed into the wagon, I asked, "Why did you bring all the dogs?"

"The pups are a month old now. Time to see the world."

Dog was lying on her side in a big wooden box. Her mouth was open with her tongue hanging out the side. The two puppies were tumbling over each other, so you could hardly tell where one pup left off and the next began. Willie B. reached in the box and lifted out the brown pup. I fished out the other one. I held his plump black belly in one hand and roughed his ears up with the other. Then I set him on my lap and pretended he was mine. I let him gnaw on my hand. "Why, he's all belly and teeth, Willie B."

He just smiled. The little lady was already asleep on his stomach, riding every breath up and down.

We got to Madison almost before we knew it. I put the black pup back in the box, and Dog licked my sleeve. I scooted to the end of the wagon and jumped down onto the dusty road. Just like before, Willie B.'s pa told us to be back by one. "And leave those pups in the wagon. Hear?"

Willie B. watched until his pa had disappeared through the door of the livery, then he pushed the bundle of pelts toward me. "You go, Jamie. I'll wait here."

"Come on, Willie B., Dog can watch her own pups for a few minutes."

"Well, hello, and look who's back." It was the storekeeper. He stopped sweeping his porch and walked over to our wagon. "I was afraid I'd seen the last of you two. What have you got there?" He looked into the box and rolled his mustache between his finger and thumb. "Pups. And it looks like they have hunting blood in their veins. What are you asking for the two of them?"

Willie B. threw a protective arm between the man and the dogs. "We aren't asking anything because they aren't for sale."

"That's too bad, Son. They look like real healthy dogs."

"They are *not* for sale. Go on in, Jamie. Sell him the skins."

I could tell he wouldn't leave his dogs alone now, so I hoisted the roll of skins onto my hip and stepped up on the walk. The storekeeper chuckled as he followed me into his store. "He's a good mother, that friend of yours."

I laid the skins out just like before, and he inspected them carefully.

"What's your name, Son?" he said.

"Jamie. James Refsell, that is."

"Well, James Refsell. I like your work, and it is a pleasure doing business with such an enterprising young man." He began to stack the skins neatly, counting as he went. "Eight, nine, and ten. Goods or cash?"

"Only ten?" I didn't care how high my voice sounded. "You're not going to buy them all?"

"I'm sorry, Jamie, but ten pelts are all I need to finish my shipment." He paused and asked again, "Goods or cash?"

As he counted the coins into my hand, he said, "I can ask if the firm wants to buy any more pelts, but I won't know for a few weeks."

I thanked him and turned for the door.

"Now I know your friend doesn't plan on selling those pups right now; but if he changes his mind, you let me know. I think I could get you a fair price for them."

Chapter 9

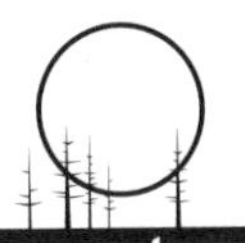

Our Last Hunt

Willie B. didn't even ask about the money or the small roll of pelts until we were out of Madison. Finally, I guess when he thought his dogs were safe, he said, "How much?"

"Two-fifty." I spat out the words. "He doesn't need any more. It isn't fair." I kicked the roll of pelts to the end of the wagon.

Willie B. was quiet for a bit. "So how much money do we have now?"

I had worked through those figures so many times, I didn't have to stop and think. "Well, five dollars for the first pelts and two-fifty today. That's seven-fifty, less forty-three cents for more shells. So that leaves us with seven dollars and seven cents. The way I figure it, we still need three dollars and ninety-one cents." I picked up the black pup and stroked his back. My anger melted into worry. "And the Parson will be back soon. Guess we better start working on what we'll tell the church."

"Don't you think we'll make it?"

I answered him like my pa would have. "Time will tell, Willie B." We each held a pup and thought our own thoughts. The wagon slowed as our fork came into view. I put the black pup back in the box and pulled the pelts over with my toe.

My pa was at the table when I came in. He had a cup of coffee and was tipped back in his chair. If he had time for coffee, it meant his work was done for the day. "How did you do, Son?"

"Two-fifty, Pa."

"Well, that's a good bit to add to your savings." He leaned forward and set his chair down on all four legs. "But you don't look very pleased about it."

I walked to the mantle and lifted down our money jar. I sat down in the chair next to Pa and dumped out the coins. I slid nickels, dimes, and pennies across the table and counted. It was just as I had told Willie B. We lacked three dollars and ninety-one cents. "It's not enough, Pa."

"True, but the money's coming in. I don't guess I see your problem." He moved his coffee cup out of his way, folded his hands, and waited.

I laid it all out the way I had it figured. "We still need six more pelts to add to the ten I brought home. And that's only good if the man at the General Store will buy them. If he won't buy them, then . . . well, I don't think we can keep our word on this, Pa."

"No, Son. You're wrong there." He wasn't mad, but his voice was hard. "If you learn nothing else from all of this, learn this much. A man must *always* keep his word." He took a deep breath. "You've got it figured out right, though. You can look for another way or you could just keep hunting on the chance he'll buy the pelts. Only six?"

He rubbed his chin and looked at me. "Just this once, I'll do your chores on Saturday, and you two get an early start hunting. Let's don't borrow trouble until we need to."

That week, school dragged by one slow day after another. Finally Mr. Golde dismissed us for the weekend. Willie B. promised he'd be ready early the next morning.

It was still dark when I rolled out of bed. I ate some cold corn bread left over from last night's supper and collected everything I'd need for the day. I shouldered Pa's rifle, strapped on my knife, and dropped extra shells into the front pocket of my overalls. Ma had made my lunch and left it on the drain board. I slipped quietly out the door and headed across the fields to Willie B.'s.

I heard their cows first, and when I rounded the bend I saw Willie B.'s pa coming from the barn with two full milk pails. "Morning, Jamie. Here he comes." Willie B. was still fastening the strap on his overalls. "Chain that dog, Son?"

Willie B. yawned before he answered. "No, sir. But she's in her pen."

"Chain her, I said. She's weaning those pups. May try to follow you."

"All right." Willie B. mumbled something and turned toward the barn. He rummaged around the harnesses, looking for a chain, and then disappeared to Dog's pen.

It wasn't long before he was back and we were off. "Couldn't find a chain, but I tied her."

My pa was right about the early start. The air was cold enough to see your breath but not cold enough to slow the rabbits yet. By the time the sun was high overhead, we had tied our jackets around our waists and each of us had rabbits dangling from our belts. We hiked to our favorite spot and stopped for lunch.

"Four rabbits, Jamie. We only need two more, and we still have all afternoon!" He grinned at me. "We'll have that Bible for Christmas."

"I hope you're right, Willie B. Done eating?"

Willie B. wiped his sleeve across his mouth and reached for the rifle. I handed it to him. He stepped quietly toward the bushes, waved me back, and without a sound began stalking. I trailed close behind and watched. He raised the gun and trained its sights on a movement that rippled along the brush. He followed the rustling branches until the animal stepped into the clearing, then squeezed the trigger.

"No!" I leaped forward and knocked the barrel away. The report of the bullet broke the stillness of the clearing, and the smell of the gunpowder stung my nose.

A furry white body tumbled down in its tracks. Dog.

We should have yelled, but neither of us made a sound. Willie B.'s arms fell heavily, with the rifle still in his hands. He didn't move; he strained to see her, but he didn't take the first step.

I don't remember how I got to Dog. I just know I was kneeling beside her; I yelled back to Willie B. "Help me!"

I watched him bend his knees and put the Winchester on the ground. Slowly and deliberately he drove himself forward one foot after the other until he stood over Dog. A piece of rope dangled from her neck; you could see where she'd chewed it. Her sides were heaving for air, and she writhed in pain. Leaves and twigs were tangled in her dirty white fur, but I couldn't see any blood. Even so, I was afraid to touch her.

"Roll her over, Willie B."

He slid his hand under her belly and gently rolled her onto her back. She yelped as he turned her over.

"Her leg, Willie B. Look, her back leg."

She'd been hit just above the knee. I looked up at Willie B. Tears were trailing down his face, but he wasn't making a sound.

"We've got to get her to my house, Willie B. It's the closest." I looked around for something. "Get that limb." I laid the rifle beside the limb and pulled my jacket from my waist. "Your jacket too, Willie B. Tie it to both sides. Now take her head. And talk to her."

Together we moved Dog onto the stretcher, and with me on one end and Willie B. on the other, we lifted the rifle and the limb and carried Dog home to Ma.

Chapter 10

Ma and Dog

Ma doesn't like to leave a chore before it's done, never has. But she left her wet laundry by the line and came on the run.

"Take her inside, Jamie."

"She's dirty, Ma, and bleeding."

"In the house, Jamie. Put her on the table and draw a basin of water. Willie B., get my basket of rags by the hearth."

I filled a basin and set it on the seat of Pa's chair. Willie B. dropped the rags into the water. Ma pulled them back out one at a time, and cleaned Dog's wound. I knew how Ma's hands felt when she set to work on an injury, and relief washed over me.

Finally Dog's leg was clean, and Ma wound a length of dry cloth around it. When she finished, Ma nodded to us, and we lifted Dog down off the table and onto a clean blanket in the washtub. We set the tub by the stove so Dog's fur could dry.

"Thank you, boys. Now you'd better go and take care of those rabbits."

The rabbits still hung heavily from our belts, so we went out to our chopping block to skin them out. When we were done, Willie B. rolled up the day's pelts and lifted the bundle. "Can I go back in and tell her good-bye?" I nodded and followed him to Ma's kitchen.

When Willie B. had finally gone, Ma put her arms around me and held me tight; I let her. My pa just said softly, "Things that hurt, teach."

I sure had learned plenty in these past few weeks. Finally I had a fire in my belly to keep my vow.

Ma kept Dog right by her stove and babied her like she did the new calves. The puppies stayed at Willie B's and seemed to do all right without Dog. But Willie B. came around every chance he got, and Dog always washed his face with her shiny pink tongue.

When Dog had been with us a week, I heard Ma talking to her as I came downstairs. I stopped to listen.

"Well, Missy. Seeing your white fur up against my stove sure shows how much it needs to be blacked. I either need to work on that stove or get you out of here."

You would've thought Dog could really understand. She yelped and pranced on her three good legs; she nipped at the hem of Ma's skirt. The stair tread I was standing on creaked and Ma looked up. "Ma, I'll black the stove for you for a quarter."

Ma laughed. "Oh, it's not so bad that I'd pay to get it done, but I do think it's time for Dog to go home. Hitch up the road cart, Jamie."

Ma held Traveler to a trot and delivered Dog home in fine style. We tied up at the rail fence. Dog whined and limped in a circle in the floor of the cart, but she didn't try to jump down. Willie B. had heard us coming, and he flew out of the house. He lifted Dog out of the cart. In the next moment Willie B. was flat on his back with his arms around Dog while the black pup jumped and danced on top of the noisy heap.

Willie B.'s ma had come out to the yard. "How's our little patient doing?"

"I'd say she's on the mend." Ma laughed.

"Then why don't you come in and celebrate?"

"Well, I guess I can for a short bit. There's plenty to do yet today, but it'll keep for a while."

Willie B. and I stayed in the yard and played with the two dogs until Dog moved off under the cart and dropped to the dirt.

"She's done in, Willie B. Let's get her to the barn."

The smells of the hay and warm livestock were just right. I hollowed out a place for Dog, and Willie B. set her gently in it. The black pup tumbled in after Dog and cuddled up beside her, and soon both were dozing.

"Where's the other pup, the little lady?" I looked around.

"Gone. Pa found a farmer out west of town who wanted her. Gave me a dollar."

"A whole dollar for a puppy?"

"And he'll pay me another quarter to train her to hunt. Pa said I can't keep her, but at least this way I can still see her. It won't be like she's truly gone, and that's another dollar and twenty-five cents for the Bible." His eyes sparkled in the dimness, and he stroked the back of the sleeping puppy.

"You made a good deal, Willie B." I reached over and cupped my hand under the black puppy's muzzle. "What about this one?"

He scooped it up with two hands and tucked it under his arm. "I can't keep him either, but I have an idea. Come on."

I stood up, knocked the hay off my britches, and followed Willie B. inside his house.

He went straight over to my ma and looked her in the eye. "Thanks for doctoring Dog for me. I can't pay you any money. Short on cash, you know." He stopped and took a deep breath. "But Jamie can have this dog. He's worth at least a dollar."

Ma looked at Willie B. with the pup, eyed him up and down. She turned and looked at me.

"Thank you, Willie B. We'll have to talk to Jamie's father."

Chapter 11

Pecans for Sale!

Pa consented—on the condition that the dog carried his weight around the farm. I would have to teach him to guard the chickens and to hunt. If I could train him, the dog was mine. Otherwise, Pa said I might as well sell him right now.

I promised that Loyal would be worth a lot to us, and I set my mind to make good on this promise.

On the Saturday after Dog had gone home, Ma was darning socks when she said, "Jamie, your pa sure would like a pecan pie. Would you go up to Olefson's and get about five pounds of pecans? There are five dimes on my dresser."

I had buttoned my coat and was ready to pull on my hat when I had an idea. "Ma?" She looked up from the sewing.

"Do the pecans have to come from the Mercantile?"

"No. I suppose not. What do you have in mind?"

"Well, I could hike out to the grove where we got them last year and get way more than five pounds. Willie B. and I could shell them. Would you pay us the same as you'd pay Mr. Olefson?"

Ma smiled. A log on the fire popped and sparks flew. "I'd say a pound of nuts shelled with love would make a tasty pie. Nuts from anywhere would be fine. Just let me know who I owe."

I pulled on my cap and ran out the door. Loyal came out of the barn on the run. Ma called, "Don't slam the—" But the door banged before I could hear the rest.

Willie B. thought it was a good idea too, and we found two empty grain sacks in his barn. Twenty-pound bags, I figured. We could sell pecans to earn the rest of the money. Two weeks till Christmas was plenty of time.

When we got to the grove, we kicked away the leaves while Loyal rolled in the piles we made. Then, on our hands and knees, we began to scoop pecans into our sacks.

"Look at all these nuts, Jamie! We'll be rich!"

In no time at all we had filled both sacks with pecans, then we easily lifted the sacks onto our backs and headed for home.

A few years back, Pa had rigged up a spring-loaded nutcracker in the barn, and we dropped our sacks beside it. I put the first nut in the trough and Willie B. tripped the spring. I scooped away the pieces and set another nut in its place.

Ping, crack, scrape. Ping, crack, scrape.

When we had a good-sized pile beneath the cracker, we stopped to comb through the shells and pick out the nut meats—but we didn't find many.

Willie B. sat back on his heels and looked at me. "What's wrong with these pecans?"

"I don't know. They look good on the outside, but the insides are all shriveled up."

We worked on in glum silence until the barn door squeaked. Ma stepped in with two steaming mugs. "Cocoa, boys? How're you doing?"

"Not so good," I said, and pointed at the heap of empty shells. Willie B. nudged the little pile of good nut meats.

"I was afraid of that, Son. Last year was real good for pecans. You can't count on two in a row." She handed us the mugs. "Put the shells out on my rose bed when you're through, and we'll see where we stand."

When the day was done, Willie B. and I gave Mr. Olefson three dimes for store-bought pecans and put the other two dimes in our jar. And we were out of business again.

Chapter 12 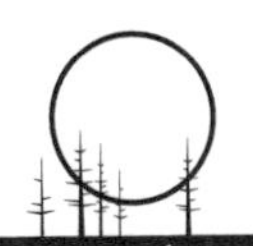

Our Last Chance

Since Willie B. was starting to train Little Lady on Saturday, I asked Pa if he could take me to Madison to try to sell the last of our pelts. The General Store seemed like our final hope.

Friday, after school, Willie B. helped me pull the nails out of the pelts. I rolled the pelts into a bundle and stuck my hands into the ends, like a muff to keep off the cold. Willie B. thumped me on the back and grinned.

All night I tossed and turned in my bed; sleep wouldn't come. The Christmas pageant was almost here, and the Parson expected to see a new Bible. The storekeeper just had to buy our pelts. I wrestled with one thought after another.

Next morning Pa hitched Traveler to the sleigh; I took Loyal along as well. Snow rested on the limbs of the trees that lined the way to Madison. It was too cold to stop and eat, so I set Loyal on the floor of the cutter and Pa handed me the reins. He lifted the basket up onto the seat between us.

When we had eaten, he handed me a tin cup. Ma had wrapped a jug of cocoa in towels, and he filled our cups from the jug.

Then he took back the reins. "Hold your cup against your cheek, Son." Pa held his own cup beneath his nose and breathed in the sweet smelling steam. "Warmth feels good, doesn't it?"

I held my cup tightly and listened to the muffled sound of runners on the snow until finally we reached Madison.

The bell on the door jingled, and the storekeeper looked up from the figures he was working on. "Well, hello. Come on in where it's warm—the dog too. He's filling out real well, isn't he?" He squatted down and watched Loyal walk right back to the stove, circle, and lie down. "And smart, I see."

He laughed, then stood up and offered his hand to Pa. "Bob Hardwell's the name. Fine boy you have there too."

Pa took his hand. "I appreciate your saying so. I'm Edward Refsell."

The man fingered his mustache. "Well, young James. What can I do for you today?"

I lifted the bundle of skins. "Last pelts of this season, sir. I was hoping you could take them this time."

"Good skins, well cleaned and trimmed, no doubt. But I'm sorry, Son, the company out east said they have all they need for now. Too bad—you came a long way to hear that." He closed his mouth so his mustache covered his lips. "Why don't you two warm yourselves by the stove a while before you go back out into the cold?"

Disappointment washed over me and I dropped the pelts onto the floor by the stove. Loyal moved himself to the top of the pile and settled down to nap again.

Pa and the storekeeper sat in the two rocking chairs by the checkerboard, and I pulled a wooden keg over and straddled it. I gazed at the red glowing edges of the stove door.

"Mr. Hardwell, how much would you pay a boy to split wood for you?"

The mustache broadened into its usual smile. "Not one thin dime, young man. Wood's plentiful in these parts, and as long as my back is strong, that's one expense I don't worry over. Tell me, Jamie. Why does a boy your age need so much cash?"

So I told the whole story about changing our world. I told it straight out and didn't lay any blame. I listed our earnings: seven dollars and fifty cents for pelts less forty-three cents for bullets, twenty cents for pecans, and one dollar and a quarter for Little Lady. "So you see, Willie B. and I, we've come up short. We still lack two dollars and forty-six cents. And if we don't make good, we have to apologize to the whole church." I felt a lump in my throat, and I tried to swallow it.

Mr. Hardwell stopped rocking and looked at me. "Do you have any other ideas?"

I'd thought about this all night, but I couldn't say it right off. "What about . . .?" I tried again. "You said you could . . . I mean, do you still think you could get a good price for . . . Loyal?"

I watched the storekeeper. He rolled the tip of his mustache between his finger and thumb. The only sounds in the whole place were the crackle of the fire in the stove and the creak of the two rocking chairs.

After a little while, he stopped his chair again, and got up. Pa and I followed him over to the counter. He stepped behind it and leafed through papers in a tray. He pulled out a tattered slip of yellow paper and held it up. "Here it is. I can sell your Loyal for seventy-five cents." A dull sound throbbed in my ears; it wasn't enough.

"But wait, maybe there's another way." He pulled out a thick catalog just like Mr. Olefson's and laid it out on top of the glass knife case. He thumbed through it and found the page with Bibles on it. Pa and I leaned over to look.

Mr. Hardwell drew his finger along the page, then stopped and pointed to one of the pictures. "Here you go, young James. A parson's Bible for eight dollars even! It has a cloth cover instead of this leather one you'd picked out, but it's a Bible all the same. What do you say? We could write up an order today and have the Bible in plenty of time for Christmas." He was pulling a tablet out of his apron pocket.

Pa straightened up and turned to me. "Well, Son? The choice is yours. You could keep Loyal this way and still have money to spare." He smiled at me.

I wanted to smile back, but I couldn't. This wasn't quite right, but I didn't know how to say it.

His smile faded. "What is it, Son?"

"Two things I guess. Seems like we should buy a leather Bible like the one we ruined; you said to repay in full measure."

"I guess I did say that."

"And then . . ." I turned back to Mr. Hardwell and looked him in the eye. "You've been real fair to me and all, but we promised Mr. Olefson we'd spend our money in his store. Guess I ought to keep that promise too. Pa says a man can keep his word, and somehow, I will."

I turned toward the stove, buttoning my coat as I went. I would sell Loyal anyway and then get out of the store fast. I picked him up, adjusted my knife, and settled him on my hip.

Mr. Hardwell closed the catalog and slid it to the side of the glass case. "Hard cash, James?"

I hoisted Loyal up on top of the knife case and rested my head on his. He twisted his face around and swiped the side of my face with his tongue. I looked down into the glass case, then my head snapped up.

"Do you trade for other goods, sir?"

"If it's worth it to me. What did you have in mind?"

"A deerfoot knife."

I was warm all over when I climbed into the sleigh beside Pa. He clucked to Traveler, and I waved at Mr. Hardwell. My other arm was wrapped around Loyal, and deep in my pocket was two dollars and forty-six cents from the sale of my knife. It would have been more, but Mr. Hardwell said the sheath could use some cleaning.

Pa reached over and stroked Loyal. I looked up at him. "It's all right about the knife, Pa. I don't figure on skinning any rabbits for a long time." He squeezed my knee, then I added, "I guess I finally changed my world for the good."

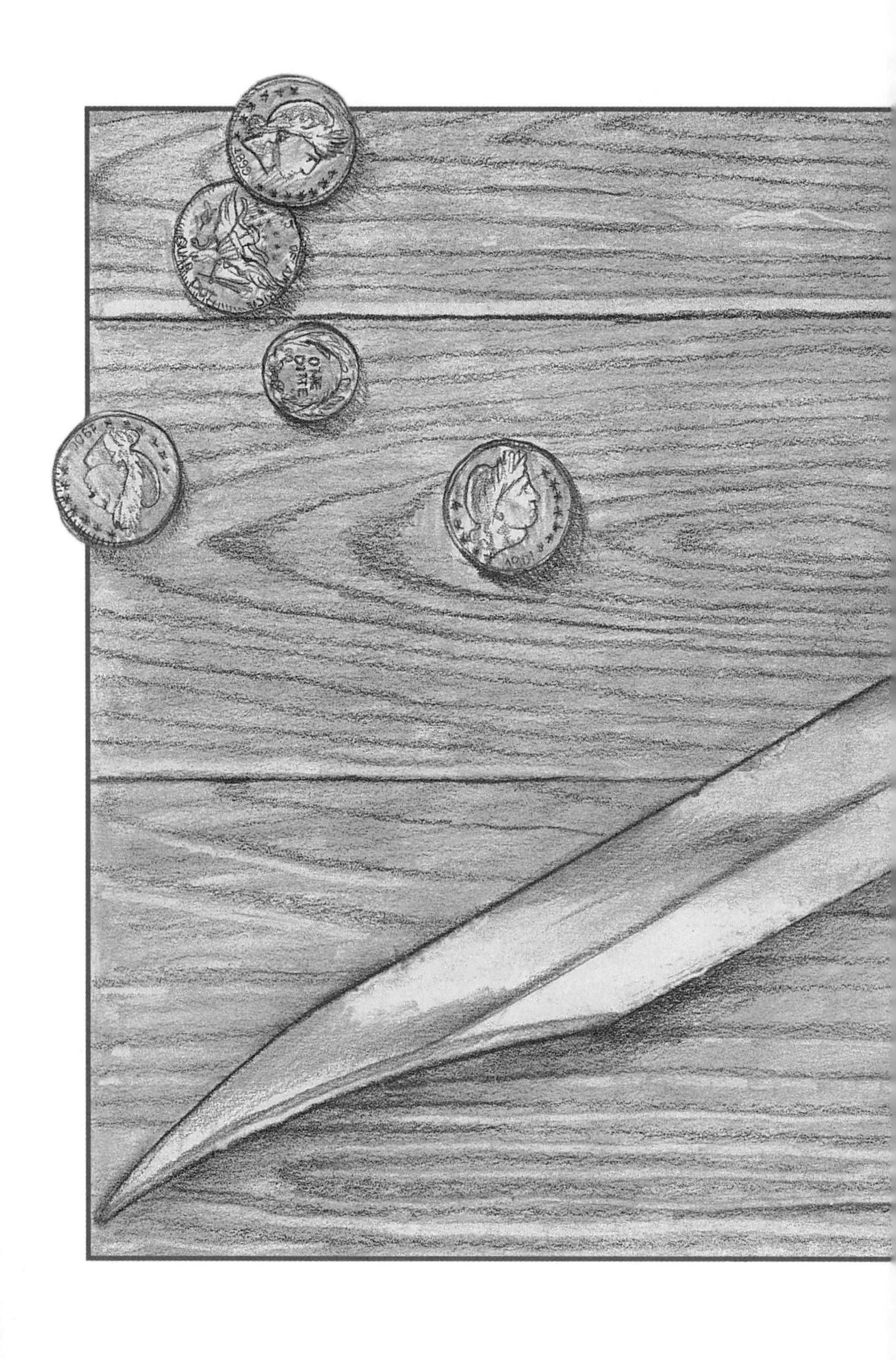

UNITED STATES OF AMERICA
CENTS
1890